Weekly Reader Children's Book Club presents

BRAVE BRUSH-TAIL POSSUM

Diane Redfield Massie

Xerox Education Publications

for Tom

Brush-tail Possum lived in the jungle
high in the green genip tree.
He slept each day curled up in a ball
in his leafy tree-fern bed.

But at night, when the stars were out,
Possum was awake. He watched the moon glide
up through the trees, lighting the leaves
below.

"I'm *not* afraid of the dark,"
said Possum. "That's because I'm so brave."
He stared at the pale, hanging vines
and shivered. The moonlight seemed to move
on the leaves. He wished he were snug in his bed.

Grey Wombat was digging,
far below, for roots under
the ferns.

"I'm *very* brave," said
Possum. "I'm as brave as
Wombat is."

"Oh, no you're not," said Wombat.
He pulled up a genip tree root and ate it.

"I'm as brave as Spiny Anteater then,"
said Possum.

"Say's who?" said Spiny Anteater,
poking her nose through the bushes.

"Well at *least* I'm as brave as Koala
Bear," whispered Possum. He bit into
a genip and sucked the sweet, sticky fruit
out of its case. The shells fell into the vines
below.

Koala Bear sat high
in the eucalyptus tree.
His fur looked silver in the
moonlight. "Yoooo hoooo!"
he called. "I'm eating leaves."

Possum watched the branches
sway gently in the breeze. The moon
was behind them, big and white.
"I'd probably be the bravest
of all," he said, "if it weren't
for the Goanna Lizard." His pale
orange eyes grew large. "If I
ever see *him* face to face,"
he whispered, "I'll freeze."

"Sneeze?" asked Koala Bear.
His mouth was full of leaves.
"He said, 'freeze,' " called Wombat,
looking up. "When he freezes,
he means he can't move. You know.
He just stands there, shaking
with fright."

"Really?" said Koala Bear.
He reached for another branch
and pulled the tender leaves
toward him. "Why doesn't he run
and jump like I do?" he asked.
"It's easy to get away."

"I can't," said Possum. "Possums can't jump."

"Why don't you dig yourself into the ground like we do?" asked Wombat. "I'm all covered up in three seconds."

"Me, too," said Spiny Anteater. "Just my quills stick out."

"I don't have paws like you have," sighed Possum. "I can't dig."

"Well, you can't just *stand* there," said Wombat.

"Yes, I can," sighed Possum.

"But you'll be eaten!" said Spiny Anteater.

"I know," said Possum.

"Don't you *care* if you're eaten?" demanded Wombat.

"Yes," said Possum,
"but I haven't any choice.
I'll freeze," he said,
"because that's what Possums
always do."

"That's terrible!" cried
Koala Bear. He slid down
the tree to a nearby branch.

"My cousins froze," continued Possum, "and *they* were eaten."

"POSSUM!" said Wombat. "You said you were *brave!*"

"I *am*," said Possum, "except for Goannas."

"Being brave means you don't just *give up*," said Wombat. He scattered dirt with his big grey feet. It sprinkled over his back.

"But my uncles and aunts . . ." said Possum. "*They* were eaten. And my great grandfather and my great grandmother, *they* were . . ."

"Never mind,"
said Wombat.
He turned around
and pushed through
the ferns. "If he won't
even *try* to save himself,"
he said, "there's nothing
we can do."
   "Oh, dear,"
sighed Spiny Anteater.
Her quills hung limply down.
   Koala Bear climbed slowly
up the eucalyptus tree. Somehow,
he wasn't hungry anymore.

Possum sat thinking alone in his tree.
The moon had scattered small patches of light
on the leaves like lizard's scales.
The Goanna's scales were white and black,
and his eyes. . . , thought Possum, were gold . . .
cold, shining eyes, ringed in gold.

Possum stood still on the genip tree
branch. He had "frozen" again.

The warm, morning sun
woke Koala Bear. He was
feeling hungry. "Hello, Possum!"
he called, chewing his favorite
leaves. The genip tree was empty.
He could see Spiny Anteater below,
looking for ants for breakfast.
"Where's Possum?" he called.

"I don't know," said Spiny Anteater.
Wombat looked out of his burrow.
He rubbed his furry nose and shook
the dust from his whiskers. "Where's
Possum?" he asked.
They stared at Possum's empty bed.
The genip tree leaves rustled softly,
making an empty sound.

"You don't suppose . . ." said Spiny Anteater. She covered her eyes with her claws. "You don't think the Goanna lizard has . . . *eaten* . . . Possum?"

"We would have *seen* the Goanna," said Wombat.

"Maybe not," sighed Koala Bear. "The Goanna lizard is very large, but he creeps so quietly over the branches."

"Possum's been eaten!" cried Spiny Anteater. "I know it! Oh, poor Possum!" Tears ran down her pointed nose and splashed on her quills beneath. "He was a *good* friend," she sobbed.

"He was the best," said Wombat, blowing his nose.

"He wasn't very brave," added Koala Bear, "but he was nice."

"I am *too* brave!" said Possum,
coming out of the bushes.

"POSSUM!" cried Spiny Anteater.
"We thought you'd been eaten!"

"Eaten?" said Possum.

"What are you doing down there
on the ground?" asked Koala Bear.

"Making something," said Possum.
He dragged some dried banana leaves
out of the grass.

'What are you making?" asked Spiny
Anteater.

"You'll see," said Possum. He spread
the banana leaves on the ground.
They looked as dry and brown as his fur.
"Now," said Possum,
"for the filling,"
and he disappeared
again through
the vines.

"What do you suppose he's making?" asked Spiny Anteater.

"Got *me*," said Wombat.

"What do you think he needs those old banana leaves for?" asked Spiny Anteater, shaking her quills.

"How should *I* know!" said Wombat. He felt cross. Spiny Anteater was always asking questions for which he had no answers.

"What's he doing *now*?" asked Spiny Anteater.

Possum backed out of the weeds. He was carrying a large bundle of something.

"What's *that*, Possum?" Spiny Anteater
stood on tip-claws to see.

"Skunk cabbages, bitter berries, stink
bugs and mud," said Possum.

"Skunk cabbages smell *terrible!*"
said Spiny Anteater.

"Bitter berries?" said Koala Bear.
"They make me sick!"

"Stink bugs," said Wombat, "Ugggggh!"

Possum dropped his bundle on the banana
leaves. Then he rolled it over and over.
"Will you help me tie the ends?" he asked.

Koala Bear found two strong vines.
He helped Possum tie the ends.

"There!" said Possum. "It's almost done."

"But what *is* it?" asked Spiny Anteater. "It looks like a sausage."

"It's not a sausage," said Possum. He dragged the stuffed banana leaves to the bottom of his tree. "When I'm finished with it," he said, "you'll know what it is." He pulled it slowly up the tree to his branch and disappeared behind the leaves.

Spiny Anteater looked at Wombat. "What do you think it's *for?*" she asked.

By late evening, Possum was out on his branch. He had found some genips for his supper.

"Yoooo hoooo! Possum!" called Koala Bear.

Possum could see Wombat and Spiny Anteater below. They were waiting next to his tree. "I've finished it," he called. "I'll bring it out."

"I can hardly wait," whispered Spiny Anteater.

Possum brought out
his stuffed banana leaves.
He propped it against the tree.
Two eyes and a nose had been
drawn near the top, and straws
poked out beneath them.

"What *is* it?" asked Wombat.

"Can't you *tell?*" said Possum.

"No," said Wombat.

"It's a sausage," said Spiny Anteater.

"IT'S *NOT* A SAUSAGE!" shouted Possum.

He sat down on the genip tree
branch and held his head
in his paws. "It's no use,"
he said.

Koala Bear slid down his tree.
"Possum," he said kindly. "Tell us
what you've made."

"It's a dummy," said Possum.
"It's a possum dummy." Tears ran
down his whiskers. "But it won't
fool the Goanna," he sighed. "He'll
know it isn't me."

"Possum," said Koala Bear.
"You were trying to save yourself.
That's very brave."

"It won't work," said Possum,
"so what does it matter? I'll
be eaten like the other possums."

"No you won't!"
said Spiny Anteater.
"It's a good dummy.
It looks just like you, Possum!"

"No, it doesn't,"
said Possum.

"At night it will," said Wombat.
"What are those things, sticking out,
supposed to be?"

"Whiskers," said Possum, sadly.

"They look *just* like whiskers,"
said Spiny Anteater, "they really do."

"I was going to set it out if the Goanna comes," sighed Possum, "and hide behind the leaves."

"That's a good idea!" said Koala Bear. "I'd like to see his face when he bites into *that!* Ugh!"

"Do you think he *might* think it's me?" Possum blew his nose.

"It's worth a chance," said Koala Bear. "It's better than freezing."

"If I look at his eyes, I might freeze anyway," said Possum.

"Don't look at his eyes," said Koala Bear.

The stars had begun to scatter themselves
about the darkening sky. Koala Bear had climbed
up to his perch, and Wombat and Spiny Anteater
were somewhere else, out of sight.

"Safe in the bushes," thought Possum. He sat
on his branch and sucked on a genip seed,
watching the silver moon.

The Goanna Lizard crawled slowly through
the trees. His pale white scales, patched
with black, matched the moon-lit leaves.
"I shall have a possum dinner," he said,
flicking his purple tongue. "Yum! Yum! Yum!"
Possum dropped his genip seed.
"It's the Goanna!" he whispered. He thought
of the Goanna's golden eyes and felt himself
turn cold. "I mustn't freeze," he said.

The Goanna Lizard crawled through
the vines. He stopped at Possum's tree.
   "AH HA!" he wheezed. "DINNER TIME!"
and he crawled onto Possum's branch.
   Possum could barely move.

"YA! YA! YOU FLABBY LIZARD!"
yelled Wombat from below.
The Goanna turned to stare.

Possum stumbled behind the leaves.
He pushed his dummy out.

The Goanna blinked
and turned around again.
He opened his scaley jaws.
SNAP! CRUNCH! His jaws
chewed up and down.

"GGGGGAAAAAAH!" he roared.
"THAT WAS POSITIVELY GHASTLY!
HORRIBLE! SICKENING! THE WORST
DINNER I'VE EVER EATEN!"
He shook his tail and shuddered.

"THAT'S THE LAST POSSUM I'LL EVER EAT!"
he bellowed, and he crawled away through
the vines.

Possum sat down on his branch.

"YOU DID IT!"
yelled Spiny Anteater,
dancing through the grass.
"YEEEEEEAAAAY for Possum!"
shouted Koala Bear. He threw
his eucalyptus leaves in the air,
and slid down his tree.

Possum smiled.
"Thanks for helping me,
Wombat," he said.
"That's O.K.," said Wombat,
chewing on a genip tree root.
"You didn't give up, even though
you were scared, and that's
really brave."
"He's as brave as I am,"
said Koala Bear.
"You're right," said Possum.
"I am."